By Brigitte Weninger

Zara Zebra Draws

Illustrated by Anna Laura Cantone

A Michael Neugebauer Book

NORTH-SOUTH BOOKS

New York/London

Zara Zebra can draw.
She draws a long, thick **line**.
What is it?
Is it a worm? Is it a stick?
Or is it a straight road?

Zara Zebra draws a big **circle**.
What is it?
Is it the sun? Is it a hoop?
Or is it a round ball?

Zara Zebra draws a **triangle**.
What is it?
Is it a magician's hat? Is it a sail?
Or is it a pointed mountain?

Zara Zebra draws a **rectangle**.
What is it?

Is it a book? Is it a bed?
Or is it a window?

Zara Zebra draws
a **square**.

On the square she puts two **circles**, a **triangle**, a **rectangle**, and one straight **line** pointing upwards. What is it?

It's a house!
Then Zara Zebra gets scissors, cuts out
one circle, and looks out of the window!